Walter Lantz®

WOODY WOODPECKER®
at the Circus

by Stella Williams Nathan
pictures by Frank McSavage

D0572838

GOLDEN PRESS • NEW YORK
Western Publishing Company, Inc., Racine, Wisconsin

F G H I J

"I feel glum, chum! I feel sad, lad!" said Woody
Woodpecker, looking first at Splinter and then at
Knothead. "We need some laughs and some fun, and
I know where we can find both! Do you know what
I've always wanted to be? A circus clown! I know I
could make people laugh! Let's go to the Crabapple
Circus and see if we can get jobs as clowns."

The very next day, Woody, Splinter, and Knothead talked about their plan with Mr. Jellyjam, owner of the Crabapple Circus.

"Everybody wants to be a clown, Woody, but it's *hard* to be funny," Mr. Jellyjam explained. "How about working with the elephants instead?"

"Well, I'd rather be a clown," declared Woody, "but taking care of elephants is a *big* job at least."

It *was* a big job.

"Gosh, Woody, pitching hay is really hot work," sighed Knothead, puffing. "I didn't know we'd have to work this hard."

"Pounding elephant stakes into the ground isn't much fun, either!" Woody complained, rubbing his beak. "Come here, Jumbo," he called to the largest elephant. "Let me straighten your chain."

Jumbo started toward Woody, but he stumbled over his twisted chain. He snorted with fright, startling Rosie, the star elephant of the circus. She tried to run, and suddenly all the elephants were tripping and stumbling together, caught in one another's tangled chains.

Mr. Jellyjam was working in a different part of the circus, but he came running when he heard the uproar.

"Elephants need to be kept *calm*, Woody," he said firmly. "I think we'd better find a new job for you and Splinter and Knothead."

"Can't we be clowns, Mr. Jellyjam?" pleaded
Woody. "I'd never be a sad lad again if I could be a
circus clown!"

"No!" Mr. Jellyjam shook his head. "You see what
you can do to help Leopold, our lion tamer."

That seemed a good idea, so off they went.

"I know how we can help Leopold," Woody told his friends. "Here's the chair he uses in his act. I'll peck some holes in the seat so he can see what the lions are doing every second!"

Splinter and Knothead agreed that this ought to be a great help.

That night, the jaunty Leopold, carrying his chair and whip, entered the lions' cage. He motioned with the chair toward Lorenzo, the boldest lion of all. Lorenzo gave the chair a big swat. *Crash!* Both Leopold and Lorenzo were stunned when the chair seat fell apart and the pieces flew across the cage.

Lorenzo leaped to the floor to examine what was
left of the chair, and Leopold scurried out of the cage.
Both of them glared at Woody, who was trying hard
to look as if a broken chair were part of the act.

"Get out!" bellowed Leopold. "Don't help me!"

"Grrow!" roared Lorenzo, just to make it clear that
he felt the same way.

Woody and the kids weren't at all surprised the following morning when Mr. Jellyjam asked, "Woody, how would you like to try something else? The trapeze act needs some help—but be careful!"

"*Can't* we be clowns, Mr. Jellyjam? Please?"

"You don't know *how* to be a good clown, Woody," Mr. Jellyjam said patiently. "You help Tina, Tom, and Terry. You tighten the trapeze ropes."

Eagerly, Woody grabbed the left rope and began to pull, hand over hand. He struggled mightily, his eyes squeezed shut with the strain.

Finally he thought, *That ought to be tight enough,* and he stopped pulling. He opened his eyes—and found himself face-to-face with Tina!

Instead of tightening the left rope, Woody had climbed it!

Woody and Tina, who was sputtering with rage, clung to the rope, helpless, until Splinter and Knothead raced in with a net. Then they dropped to safety. The relieved audience cheered, and Mr. Jellyjam hurried over.

"Hey, kids," shouted Woody, "listen to that crowd! Our chance to be clowns has come at last."

But Mr. Jellyjam shook his head. "I'm sorry, Woody. I know you have worked hard, but you make just too many mistakes. You can feed the trained dogs if you want to—you can't do any harm there—but that's the only job left that I can give you."

They were very disappointed, but Woody, Splinter, and Knothead did like the playful pooches in the dog act. That evening, they waited at ringside with a good supply of dog biscuits.

"Here, puppies! Have a treat!" Woody tossed a handful of biscuits to the performers.

Excited, the dogs started running and jumping all around the ring. While the band music played, the dogs raced around wildly. Woody, Splinter, and Knothead were knocked head over heels.

Frenchy, a poodle, scrambled up a ladder. Woody jumped to his feet and raced after him, but the poodle leaped onto a small swing just as Woody reached for him. With a frightened whoop, Woody lost his balance and fell off the ladder.

Meanwhile, Susie the terrier had jumped up onto the back of a pony waiting its turn to perform. The pony broke into a gallop. Splinter and Knothead grabbed the pony's tail, and Woody, tumbling from the ladder, landed on the racing pony's back. But Susie was just out of reach.

Mitzie, the star toy poodle, pranced in front of the three hoops that she usually jumped through in her act. She leaped through the first hoop. Woody slid from the pony's back and tried to follow her through the tiny colored hoop. He didn't make it! Max the beagle, balancing on his rolling red barrel, crashed into Woody, pushing the woodpecker partway through the second and third hoops as well.

Woody looked up from his trap of hoops and saw Mr. Jellyjam standing in front of him.

"Oh, I'm sorry!" he gasped. "I'm really sorry. I guess I'd better quit—"

"Listen!" Mr. Jellyjam interrupted. "Listen to the crowd *this* time, Woody!"

Woody listened, and he heard laughter and cheering such as he had never heard before. The audience thought the blunders had been all part of the act—and they loved it!

"Woody, you were right," Mr. Jellyjam said. "I was wrong. You are a *wonderful* clown. Oh, how you can make people laugh!"

Happily, Woody bowed to his cheering fans.
"Thank you, Mr. Jellyjam." He turned to Knothead
and Splinter. "Don't be sad, lad! Don't be glum,
chum! We're clowns in the circus now. And what a
great life it's going to be—making people laugh!"